W9-AAD-079

WOLF HIGH

by P.W. Hueller

12 STORY LIBRARY

www.12StoryLibrary.com

Copyright © 2015 by Peterson Publishing Company, North Mankato, MN 56003. All rights reserved. No part of this book may be reproduced or utilized in any form or by any means without written permission from the publisher.

12-Story Library is an imprint of Peterson Publishing Company and Press Room Editions.

Produced for 12-Story Library by Red Line Editorial

Photographs ©: Shutterstock Images, cover, 3

Cover Design: Emily Love

ISBN
978-1-63235-055-8 (hardcover)
978-1-63235-115-9 (paperback)
978-1-62143-096-4 (hosted ebook)

Library of Congress Control Number: 2014937422

Printed in the United States of America
Mankato, MN
June, 2014

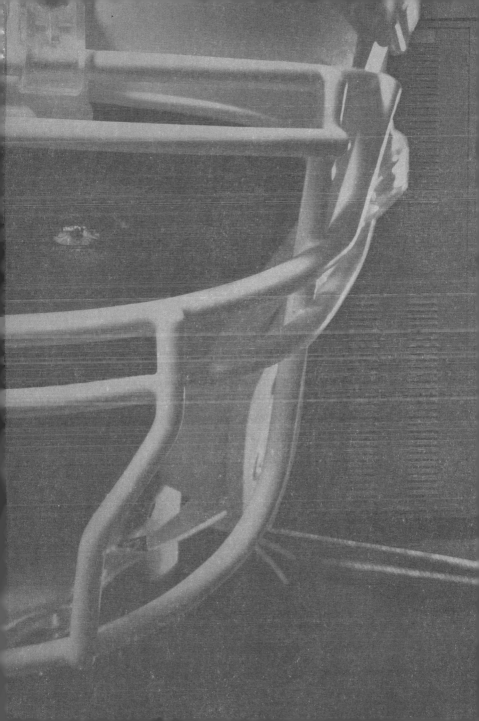

CHAPTER

1

By now, you probably know a lot about werewolves. You've sat next to one in school. You've watched a friend suddenly grow fur and fangs. You've heard them growl as they roam the halls between classes.

Even if you haven't experienced these things, you've no doubt seen them on TV. When werewolves aren't scoring touchdowns or slamming down dunks, they're starring in commercials for sports cars and sports drinks.

According to my mom, there was a time when movies were the only places people saw werewolves. That was before we knew they actually existed. Before they actually *did* exist.

Back then, calithrene, aka Wolf-It!©, hadn't yet hit the market. One time, I asked my mom where Wolf-It!© comes from. She said it's a complex compound that can be extracted from a wolf's digestive system. Whatever that means. She helped invent the stuff, so I'll take her word for it.

Athletes quickly discovered that one gulp of Wolf-It!© helped them gain an extra yard on the football field or add an extra inch to their vertical jump. They realized that regular use made them run faster and jump higher than any person had ever run or jumped before.

After all, Wolf-It!© didn't just improve athletes. It changed them.

Genetically.

They were faster than human beings because they were no longer fully human.

It took awhile for everyone to start calling them werewolves. They didn't look like creatures from horror flicks. For one thing, their transformation had nothing to do with the moon. Despite the fangs and the fur, they appeared more human than wolf. They walked on two legs. They had hands and feet instead of paws. They even kept going to school, kept wearing clothes, and after some controversy—kept playing sports.

But you already know all this.

What you don't know is what it feels like to be one of them. To feel that strength. That rage. That predatory urge to rip something to shreds.

I do. Because I have a secret. One that I've never told anyone.

I am a werewolf.

CHAPTER
2

"Alex!" my mother says, knocking on the bathroom door. That's my name—Alex Hughes. "You're going to be late for school."

"I'm coming," I tell her.

There's a pause. Then Mom asks, "Is everything okay?" Her voice is quiet, concerned.

"Yeah, Mom," I tell her, even though we both know it isn't. She's the only other person who knows what's happening to me. "I'm just shaving."

What else is new? Lately, I've been shaving three or even four times a day. Chin stubble is one thing—but forehead stubble? It'd be a dead giveaway. Pretty soon I'll have to bring a razor with me to school.

I look at myself in the mirror for a while longer. My eyes are red and have bags under them. It's getting harder and harder to sleep at night. The urge to jump out my window and roam the neighborhood is almost overpowering.

"Alex!" Mom says, snapping me out of my thoughts. "Let's go!"

"Coming!"

CHAPTER
3

"Not hungry?" Mom says.

"Not for *that*," I tell her, pointing to the bowl of cereal with my spoon. "How about some bacon?"

The anger in my voice scares her. "Your condition, it's getting worse, isn't it?" she says.

I hate it when she calls it that. *My condition*. As if I'm sick or something.

"You know it is," I grunt. "That's why you hide the pills in my cereal."

"I'm not hiding anything, Alex." Mom's voice is full of concern. "I put them in the cereal so they're easier to eat. I told you that."

This is true. She *did* tell me about the pills. Just like she told me that the pills slow down "my condition." She's explained to me that they're not a cure, but they give her more time to find one. If my best friend, Harry, knew I was taking these pills he'd call me crazy. Why would I want to slow down the changes that were happening to me? Why wouldn't I want to be stronger and faster than everybody else? Why wouldn't I want to become rich and famous? Who in their right mind wouldn't want to be a werewolf?

My mom rests her hand on my shoulder. As if she's reading my mind, she tells me, "I know you're having doubts. But that's part of your condition. Fight it, Alex. Please, *please* fight it. Remember all the bad stuff that's going to happen to you if we don't fix this. Remember what happened to your father."

That's the thing. I don't remember Dad. Never have. I was four, almost five, when he finally died, but I can't picture him. Mom says I must have blocked him out. She says his memory must be too traumatic for me to deal with.

I watch her dig through my cereal bowl with her fingers until she finds the pill.

"Please?" she says again.

Before I know what I'm doing, I lick the pill right out of her palm and swallow.

CHAPTER
4

By the time I arrive at school, the pill is doing its job. I feel more clear-headed. I feel like myself again.

Mom's right. There's a lot of bad stuff that goes with being a werewolf. We may gain strength and speed, but we lose a lot, too. Our friends. Our personalities. Our self-control.

Even our ability to talk.

Then, after we have lost pretty much everything that matters, we lose our lives.

The average life span of a werewolf is less than 40 years. Mom thinks it's only going to get worse. She says the human body was never meant to deal with the effects of Wolf-It!©. And what about those of us who were born with the condition? It may have taken puberty to trigger our fur and fangs, but we have an early death written into our DNA.

Not that anyone cares. Mom says people never feel sorry for the rich and famous. Especially when there are even richer people who make their money by hiding the truth from the rest of us.

"That's why we need to hide the truth from *them*," Mom always says. "If they found out about you . . . "

She never needs to finish that sentence. I agree. If people knew what I was, everything would change. Which is why I shave every morning (and afternoon, and in the middle of the night). And why I file down my fangs once a week. When I'm thinking straight, I know I don't want to be a wolf. I want to be human. I want to be me.

Still, I know the pills are only a temporary fix. Their effects are beginning to wear off faster and faster. I'm lucky to make it through an entire day feeling like myself. At some point, they'll stop working altogether.

When that happens, I'll become just like Nick Jackson.

I'm at my locker when he arrives this morning. The hallway is crowded with other students, so I hear Nick before I see him. He's snarling and growling as usual.

As always, Nick's not alone. Werewolves prowl in packs. At Sutherland High—that's the name of my school—there are five (known) werewolves. Three guys, two girls. They go everywhere together. They eat lunch at the same otherwise empty table. They sit next to each other in every class. Trying to keep them separate for even one period was just too much work. Especially before the teachers were armed with tranquilizer guns.

Nick is the pack leader. All werewolves are aggressive, but Nick? He's vicious. His white-blond hair bristles. His blue eyes bounce all over the place. His jaws snap as his lips curl.

The other students look down. They know it's not safe to meet Nick's eyes. The only time it's safe to look at Nick is when he's on the football field. Assuming you're not on the field with him, that is.

That's when I notice the one student who isn't looking away. He's super scrawny—a freshman, probably—but that's no excuse. Not if Nick notices him. The kid is five or six lockers away, and I start to edge my way toward him. If I can get to him in time, I can get him out of harm's way.

But I don't. I hardly make it more than a foot or two before Nick pounces on the kid, fangs bared.

It's impossible to see what happens after that. The other werewolves group around Nick as two hall monitors empty their tranquilizer guns. The darts sink into the wolves' backs, and they fall, unconscious, to the floor. The hall monitors tell everyone to stay back as they pull the wolves off the pile. This is slow work. Most of the wolves weigh well over 200 pounds.

The bell for first period rings, but none of the kids go to class. Now that the wolves have been knocked out, students aren't afraid to watch.

They want to see if the freshman is still alive.

CHAPTER
5

We don't get a good look at the freshman until the hall monitors lift Nick off him. They set Nick next to the other unconscious werewolves then hurry back to the unconscious kid. One of the hall monitors puts two fingers on the freshman's neck, checking for a pulse. He nods to the other hall monitor. The freshman is alive, but just barely.

Blood is everywhere. Before he got tranquilized, Nick must have bitten into the boy's shoulder, because the kid's shirt is torn and seeping fresh blood.

The hall monitors carefully pick up the kid. They take him down the hall and out the door, where an ambulance is likely already waiting.

"What was that kid thinking?" a familiar voice says.

I turn to find Harry, my best friend, standing next to me. As usual, he's wearing his letter jacket—even though he hasn't lettered in anything. It has a big white *S* stitched onto the front, but that's it. No basketball or football patches. I've tried again and again to convince him to join the debate team; he's such a good talker, he'd definitely get a patch in debate.

It took him years to save up enough money to buy the jacket, even though he's been working 40 hours a week since he was 14 years old. (He lied about his age on the application.) He gives most of the money he makes to his mom, who works two jobs herself just to make ends meet.

"He didn't know," I say.

"How could he not know? *Everyone* knows you don't look them in the eyes. Werewolves are totally harmless unless you look them in the eyes."

This is a standard belief about werewolves. It's been repeated by principals on loudspeakers and by parents to their children. But if adults really believe that, why are so many of them armed with tranquilizer guns? It's not just the hall monitors; it's everyone.

The hall monitors have come back for the still-unconscious werewolves. They'll take the wolves down to the new and improved nurse's station. Over the summer, the station was expanded to include several rooms that lock from the outside. Video cameras were also installed. Now the nurse can monitor the werewolves from the safety of her office.

"I just hope that kid's antics don't get Nick suspended from tomorrow's game," Harry says.

"That's really what you're thinking about right now?" I ask him. "Tomorrow's game?"

A kid was almost killed right in front of us, I think. *How could anyone, let alone my best friend, be worrying about tomorrow's game?*

Then again, I don't know why I'm surprised. Tomorrow's football game is going to be nationally televised. It's all *anyone* at my high school is thinking about. Sutherland High is one of the poorest schools in one of the poorest districts in the state. Our textbooks are often two or three decades old. I don't know how funding gets distributed, but it sure feels like it never finds its way to Sutherland. It feels like we've been completely forgotten.

Until now.

Thanks to Nick and the other males in his pack, our football team is ranked second in the state. Tomorrow, we play the number one team: Eagle Valley. Our school has been swarmed by reporters all week. They've sat in the bleachers during practice. They've interviewed our principal, our coach, and even some of the players. They've put Sutherland on the map.

Harry was even interviewed. He guaranteed on national TV that we would win tomorrow's game. So I can understand why he's worried that our star player won't be allowed to play.

"You're just jealous," he says to me. "You think you should be the one getting all the attention instead of Nick."

"You really think I'm jealous?"

"I'm not saying I blame you," Harry says. His voice softens with sympathy. "If my dad was Terry the Terror, I'd be jealous, too. What are the odds that you'd get your mom's genes instead of your dad's?"

Did I mention my dad was a professional football player? And not just any professional football player, either. He was the very first football player to use Wolf-It!©, and the very first to get suspended for using it, too.

I think that's one of the reasons Harry became my friend. He felt sorry for me. My dad was one of the most famous werewolves in America, but as far as Harry could tell, my dad hadn't passed on his genes to me. In Harry's eyes, I was just about the unluckiest person on the planet.

I honestly don't think we'd be friends if I told him the truth. *I did get my dad's genes, Harry, but I don't want them. In fact, I'm doing everything I can not to be a werewolf.* If he knew that, he'd go from feeling sorry for me to thinking I was absolutely insane.

Of course, he's going to learn the truth soon enough. As we watch the hall monitors take away the last of the knocked-out werewolves, I think about my mom and her attempts to find a cure.

She better find one quick, I think. And as I think this, I can't help imagining the hall monitors carrying me away, too.

CHAPTER
6

During sixth period, all of the werewolves return to class except Nick. Is he actually going to get suspended? Unlikely. Maybe he got shot by more darts than the others and hasn't woken up yet.

Actually, that's what most of the werewolves are doing right now. Sleeping. They're sitting in their desks at the front of the classroom, snoring.

This isn't unusual. That's what they spend most of the day doing. Mr. Hamilton, our math teacher, doesn't dare wake them. He just talks over their snores, his hand resting on his tranquilizer gun.

For some reason, the two female werewolves don't sleep as much during class. Especially Tamara Chaney. I swear, sometimes when I watch her, it looks like she's actually paying attention to the teacher. I realize that's impossible. Werewolves don't care about school—everybody knows that.

As far as I can tell, Tamara doesn't even care that I exist.

But that doesn't stop me from staring at her long, wild auburn hair as much as possible.

After all, I'm in love with her.

I'm not alone. Who isn't in love with werewolves these days? Thanks to the females' toned legs and lustrous hair, each one of them looks like a supermodel. No wonder so many of them star in shampoo commercials. As I watch Tamara scratch her side, I know I'm not the only guy taking a peek at her briefly exposed midriff.

But there's a difference between me and the other guys. They all fell in love with Tamara after she became a werewolf. I loved her before, back when she did care that I existed. Back when I called her Mara. When we were best friends.

Back then, her hair was always in a ponytail. She was the fastest girl in school, not to mention the smartest. She beat me at pretty much everything, whether it was a math quiz or a game of H.O.R.S.E. And I didn't mind a bit. Back then, I thought she was destined to be the biggest sports star in the school. How could I have known that she'd willingly give up playing sports? How could I have known that she'd turn into a werewolf?

Mara was in love, too. But not with me.

The classroom door slams open. Nick Jackson shuffles into the room. He's still drowsy from the tranquilizer darts. Drowsy and angry. He snaps his jaws at Mr. Hamilton before taking his seat at the front of class. Nick's white hair bristles.

Why did Mara have to fall in love with *him*?

CHAPTER
7

I'm a little late to football practice. That's what happens when you have to shave your forehead in a public locker room without anyone noticing.

Anyway, it's not like anyone cares that I'm late. Sometimes I think that Coach Leonard doesn't even know I'm on the team. The only players he seems to care about are the werewolves. After all, they're going to win him a state championship.

I play middle linebacker, the same position my dad played. The same position Nick Jackson plays. In other words, I don't so much *play* middle linebacker as stand on the sideline and watch Nick play middle linebacker.

He's on the field now, grunting and growling. Everyone else is trying to take it easy. They don't want to get injured before the big game. But Nick's not capable of taking it easy. When Jake, our running back, takes a hand-off and jogs up the field, Nick launches himself in the air and smashes into him. Jake quickly goes limp. That's what we've all learned to do when getting tackled by a werewolf. Don't resist. Don't fight for an extra yard. Werewolves hate that.

As usual, Nick's not wearing his helmet. That's another thing about werewolves—for some reason, they won't wear their helmets. Other than tranquilizing them, there's no way to make them. Early on, there was some public outcry about head injuries. But that went away when people realized how much more entertaining the game was when you could see the werewolves' faces. In NFL and college games, they often plant a mic in a werewolf's jersey or shoulder pads. That way people watching on TV can hear the snarls that go along with the dilated nostrils, the pulled-back ears, and the chomping jaws.

Plus, since werewolves can't talk, networks don't need to worry about them cussing on live TV.

I bet NSBC (National Sports Broadcasting Channel) will plant a mic in Nick's shoulder pads for tomorrow's game. He's the main reason they're showing this game. He's the reason reporters have traveled across the country to be here. He's the reason some NSBC technicians are currently trying to fix our scoreboard. It's been broken for the last three seasons; our school board hasn't had the money to fix it. Now they won't need to. NSBC wants everything to look as good as possible for the viewers at home.

Then again, maybe they'll mic up Harry. He's sitting in the stands with a bunch of reporters and answering their questions. He may not be much of an athlete, but he's always been good at talking. If they gave him a microphone, he'd probably give an entertaining play-by-play. I can't hear him from this distance, but I know him well enough to imagine the conversation he's having. He's probably saying, "The Eagle Valley offense better bring their jackets. It's going to be cold and they're going to be standing on the sidelines most of the game." Harry should be one of those guys who promote boxing or wrestling matches. He's the best trash talker I know.

I watch him open and close his mouth and wave his hands around to make another point. The reporters are hanging on his every word. Then, suddenly, Harry points to the field. All the reporters look to where he's pointing. So do I.

It takes me a second, but I finally see what Harry saw. There's a mouth guard lying on the 50-yard line. Not just any mouth guard, either. A heavy-duty mouth guard that protects both the top and bottom teeth.

It's a FangGuard©.

Werewolves might not have to wear helmets, but they do have to wear FangGuards©. If they didn't, they'd sink their teeth into other players' flesh every chance they got.

Why non-werewolves use FangGuards© is a mystery. I guess they think they look cool or something.

Anyway, whenever a mouth guard ends up on the field, people panic. Especially when there's a pile of players next to it. If the FangGuard© belongs to a werewolf, someone in the pile is probably being eaten.

We all wait anxiously while Coach Leonard and his assistant coaches try to clear the pile. Truthfully, there's not much they can do. The tranquilizer darts are too potent to use on a non-werewolf. That means they can't start shooting until they have an easy shot.

One by one, players get up and back away from the pile.

I'm trying to see if there's blood on the field, but other players are standing in the way.

When the coaches get to the bottom of the pile, Nick Jackson and another player are at the bottom. The coaches pull Nick to his feet. Or they try to. He shrugs them off and snarls.

Oh, no, I think. *Not again.*

Is he wearing his FangGuard©? Is there blood dripping from his chin?

I breathe a sigh of relief.

Yes, Nick's wearing his mouth guard. It's Jake who isn't. Nick must have tackled him so hard it popped out.

I look back at Harry in the stands. He's pointing right at me.

He's probably telling the reporters who I am—who my father was.

He's probably telling them that my dad is the reason they invented FangGuards©.

My dad—Terry the Terror. The first werewolf to kill someone in front of a national TV audience.

CHAPTER
8

When I get home after practice, Mom's nowhere to be found. This isn't unusual. As a lead scientist at H.O.W.L., she often works long hours. (H.O.W.L. stands for the last names of the lab's founding members: Hughes, Orr, and Williams. The 'L' just means *Lab*, I guess. There were actually several other founding members, but they agreed H.O.W.L. was a lot more catchy than H.O.W.B.T.N.R.G.L.)

What *is* unusual is that Mom didn't tell me she'd be late. There's no note on the kitchen counter. I check my phone for messages. Nope. No text. No voicemail.

I try calling her, but she doesn't answer.

Truthfully, I'm kind of glad she isn't home yet. After our conversation this morning, she probably wants to talk about how I'm feeling. That's pretty much all we ever talk about these days. I understand her concern, but right now I have other things on my mind.

Like the close call on the football field today.

Like my father.

I head upstairs and into Mom's office. I boot up the computer and do an online search for "Terry the Terror Hughes."

This isn't the first time I've done this. In fact, it's about the thousandth. All the same links and pictures pop up. When I said I can't remember my father, I didn't mean I couldn't remember what he looked like.

Everybody knows what Terry the Terror looked like.

Picture after picture shows him standing over players he's just tackled. His mouth is always open wide. His fangs are always bared.

These are the pictures that made my dad famous. In one offseason he went from benchwarmer to superstar. He went from man to werewolf.

My father, as everybody knows, was the first to do a lot of things. He was the first werewolf, the first player to refuse to wear a helmet, the first American football player to be famous all over the world. As popular as football has always been in the US, it never caught on in the rest of the world until my father took off his helmet.

His snarling face could be seen on TVs and billboards across the globe.

In other words, my dad was H.O.W.L.'s first patient. I'm still not exactly sure how he and my mother met. Did they start dating before she began developing Wolf-It!© or after? I've asked Mom about this, but she doesn't like to talk about it. It's too painful for her.

At the time, they weren't doing anything illegal. Wolf-It!© was meant to be an organic supplement. After Dad's success with it, you could buy it over the counter in any store.

Not for long, though.

Within a few months, Dad wasn't alone. Werewolves were everywhere. In schools. In advertisements. On every sports court and field.

It's actually amazing that Dad was the first werewolf to kill someone on national TV. In the weeks that followed, it became clear that werewolf-related deaths were happening all over the place. Why these deaths weren't reported is complicated. At least that's what my sixth-grade history teacher, Mr. Collins, told me.

When I asked my mom, she laughed bitterly. "It's not complicated at all," she said. "They weren't reported because no one cared."

"How could no one care?" I asked her.

"We were having too much fun watching werewolves. So long as it wasn't our loved ones who were dying, we didn't care."

Besides, she told me, it was mostly professional athletes and poor kids who bought Wolf-It!©.

"Why poor kids?" I asked her.

My mom's answer to that question was to enroll me at Sutherland Middle School. She wanted me to see the answer for myself. She wanted me to see what poverty looked like. What hunger looked like. She wanted me to see kids who were lucky if they got one meal a day. Unlike most of the other students, I quickly realized, I truly was lucky. I didn't have to worry about when I was going to eat again. I could give away my lunch to others because I knew dinner would be waiting for me when I got home. I didn't have to get a job, like Harry and so many others did, because my mom already had enough money to keep the water running and the heat on.

So most people didn't care about the true danger of werewolves until the referees cleared a pile of football players and found my father chomping away. The player he was eating lay in a pool of his own blood.

I click on one more image. It's the image everyone thinks of when they think of my father. A droplet of blood hangs from one of his fangs.

For months, this image was everywhere. It flashed onto the screen during Dad's trial. League officials held it up for everyone to see as they announced that werewolves were banned from playing sports. Politicians showed the image as they declared Wolf-It© to be an illegal substance.

My mom took the stand at my father's trial. She said that my father wasn't to blame; he had no way of knowing that Wolf-It© would make him so violent. No one did. H.O.W.L. had gone through all the proper steps when they invented Wolf-It!©. They had let the medical community give the substance a thorough examination. They'd even run non-human tests. But there was no real way to anticipate the effects of Wolf-It!© on people.

The court must have agreed with her. Neither Mom nor Dad went to jail. Dad was placed under house arrest. That's where he died—in our home—a few years later.

I was born right after the trial. It wasn't until my generation reached puberty that werewolves became popular again. People had to decide what to do with these teenagers who were suddenly sprouting fangs.

Some thought we should be gathered up and locked away. Others thought it was unfair to punish us for our parents' decisions. According to Mr. Collins, the people fighting for werewolf rights eventually won

Once again, my mom had a different point of view. "I wish I could tell you that werewolves were given equality because it's the right thing to do," she said. "But I'd be lying. The only reason they're treated equally is plain and simple greed."

According to my mom, people quickly realized that they could make money off of werewolves. Instead of looking for a cure, politicians and sports officials worked together to invent the FangGuard©. While Wolf-It!© is still illegal, sports leagues no longer test for it.

While the rest of H.O.W.L. continued to sell Wolf-It!© on the black market, my mother has spent the last decade trying to invent a cure. Mom says she can't possibly make up for the lives she ruined, but at least she can prevent other lives from being ruined in the future.

H.O.W.L. claims publicly that they make other, legal supplements—which is true. But Wolf-It!© is still far and away their best-selling product.

My phone rings. It's Harry.

"Dude," he says. He's calling from Burger Hut, where he works. "We got someone's order wrong. Want some free burgers?"

It's only then that I realize I haven't eaten dinner yet.

"On my way," I tell Harry.

I look at the image of my father's bloody mouth one more time. Then I turn off the computer and make my way to the door. I'm a block down the road when I realize I should probably call Mom and let her know where I'm going.

But once again, she doesn't pick up.

CHAPTER
9

I see Harry before he sees me. I don't try to get his attention, because I like to watch him work.

Does that sound weird?

If it does, that's just because you've never seen someone so good at their job.

Harry's only 17, but he's already been the manager of Burger Hut for a year. It didn't take his boss long to realize Harry had what he likes to call "a gift for gab."

In other words, that kid can talk.

Tonight Harry's standing behind a register, fitting in some small talk while he takes a bald guy's order. "You again!" he says. "Larry, right? I said you'd be back, didn't I? No one bellies up to this burger bar just once. People from the South talk with a drawl. People at Burger Hut eat with a drool."

The guy just nods his head and laughs. He's not alone. Everybody in the restaurant is doing the same thing. By now, Harry's a local celebrity. People go to Burger Hut as much to hear him talk as to eat burgers.

As usual, Harry's not just working the cash register. He wears a headset so he can talk to the drive-thru customers as well. After taking the bald guy's order, he lifts the microphone closer to his mouth. "Welcome to Burger Hut," he says, "where your taste buds become our taste *buddies*."

Harry is still talking when he notices me standing by the fountain drinks. He finishes the order, takes off the headset, and grabs a bag of burgers from behind the counter.

"Let's eat them out back," he says to me.

"Out back?" I ask. Harry's been "accidentally" getting orders wrong for years, and we always eat them in the restaurant.

"I could use some fresh air," he says. He reaches behind the counter again and pulls out his letter jacket without a letter.

I shrug my shoulders. The walk from my house to the restaurant was really cold. I'm only now starting to thaw. But then again, free burgers are free burgers.

We walk out of Burger Hut together and make our way around the restaurant. When Harry said he wanted to meet out back, he wasn't kidding. He sits down on some asphalt next to the Dumpster.

"Not sure this air is going to be fresh," I say.

The Dumpster is so full the lid can't close all the way.

"Thought it would be easier to talk out here," he says. He takes a burger out of the bag and hands it to me.

"You were talking pretty well in there," I say. I take the burger and sit down next to him.

Even though Harry said he wanted to talk about something, we don't. We sit there and munch on our burgers. That's okay with me. I don't think I realized how hungry I was until I started eating. Mom and I usually eat dinner around 6:00, but it must be 8:30 by now. The sky is pitch black.

I finish one burger and check my phone.

Still no messages from Mom.

As I look at the phone, I reach into the bag to grab another burger. But what I pull out of the bag isn't a burger. It's a small, clear, plastic bottle. The liquid in the bottle is also clear.

"What is this?" I ask Harry.

"You know what it is," he says.

He's right. I do. It's a bottle of Wolf-It!©.

CHAPTER
10

"Where'd you get this?" I ask Harry.

He's smiling from ear to ear. "It wasn't easy," he says. "I had to follow Nick Jackson for weeks before I figured out where he tossed his empties." He pauses to let this sink in. *Nick Jackson uses Wolf-It!©. That means he's not a hereditary werewolf!* For most people, this would be shocking news. Not me, though. I've known for years that Nick's a cheater. "Turns out he just throws them in the Dumpster by his house," Harry tells me. He taps the Dumpster with his knuckles. "Each bottle had a little bit left in it—a few drops, tops. It took me months to gather enough."

"Enough for what?" I ask.

"Enough for each of us." Harry reaches in the bag and takes out another bottle.

We sit there for a while in silence. I stare at the bottle I'm holding and try to think of something to say. But I can't think of anything. I'm too surprised to think.

"Cheers," Harry says. He tries to clink his bottle against mine, but I don't let him.

Finally, my mouth works. "I can't drink this, Harry."

He's still smiling. "It's okay. Really. I want you to have it. Look, one bottle won't be enough to turn you into a werewolf, but maybe you can get an extra boost for tomorrow's game."

I think about Harry risking his life day after day to get this stuff—not just one bottle but two. One for him. One for me. I think about what a great friend he's being.

It would be so easy to clink bottles with him. Two or three swallows and the bottle would be empty.

Besides, he's right. Taking Wolf-It!© one time doesn't make you a werewolf. According to my mom, it took Dad weeks to grow his fangs.

Then again, she says the stuff they make today is more potent. More dangerous. Mom says that overdosing is more common than ever.

"I'm sorry, Harry," I tell him. "I just can't."

Harry's smile vanishes. "What are you talking about? Why not?"

"Because . . ." I say, but my voice trails off. Why can't I take Wolf-It!©? Because I'm already a werewolf. And because I promised my mother. And because, frankly, I'm worried that she's in trouble. She's secretly trying to find a cure for something no one wants cured. What if the other H.O.W.L. employees found out? What would they do?

I can already feel my mind starting to get cloudy. The pill I took this morning must be wearing off. I need to keep my head as clear as possible for as long as possible.

Of course, I can't tell Harry any of this. So instead I say, "You shouldn't take it, either."

Harry's eyes are wild with disbelief. "You can't be serious. Do you know how long it took me to get this? This stuff can change our *lives*, Alex."

No, I tell myself, *it can ruin our lives.* I already lost my dad to Wolf-It!©. Then I lost Mara. I don't even want to think about what could happen to Harry. One dose won't turn him into a werewolf, but it is enough to alter a person's genetics. What if his personality changes? What if . . .

"Your voice," I say. "What if you lose your voice?"

Harry laughs bitterly. "Then I won't have to work here anymore," he says. "I'm sick of putting on a show for people on the off chance they'll give me a $2 tip."

Before I can stop him, he tilts his head back and pours the clear liquid down his throat. He grimaces and gives me one more chance to drink from the bottle I'm still holding.

"Suit yourself," he says.

Harry rips the bottle out of my hand and once again tilts his head back.

CHAPTER
11

"No!" I yell.

But of course I'm too late.

"What are you doing?" I scream. "Why did you do that? Don't you know you can't take two bottles in one day?"

Everyone knows that. Even when Wolf-It!© was a legal substance, they only allowed you to buy one bottle at a time. There are only so many ounces of that stuff a body can take at once.

Harry doesn't seem to be able to hear me screaming at him. He's shaking violently. I know I should call 911, but I'm using both arms to keep Harry from falling.

I feel helpless. So I just keep screaming "Why?" over and over.

Harry stops shaking. I have my arms wrapped around his perfectly still body. "Harry?" I say. "Are you okay?"

I'm just about to step back and look at him when I hear him growl. He shoves me to the ground.

Then he takes off running.

CHAPTER
12

As I watch Harry run away, I again consider calling 911. If I told them my buddy just downed two bottles of Wolf-It!©, they'd send an ambulance as fast as possible.

But where would they send it? Harry is already just a speck in the distance. Who knows where he'll be by the time an ambulance arrives.

Besides, if I call 911, the police will have to get involved. Taking Wolf-It!© is illegal. Do I really want to get my best friend arrested?

The only other thing I can think to do is to chase after him. I have no idea what I'm going to do if I catch him, but at least I'll be doing *something*.

I run across the parking lot and down the street. I sprint past one run-down apartment building after another. I'm on the sidewalk, pumping my arms.

But it doesn't matter. I lost sight of Harry blocks ago. That dude is *fast*. As long as I've known him, Harry has always looked funny running. He's waddled around like a penguin. Now he lopes like a wolf.

I don't know where Harry is or where he's planning to go. I have no idea what to do.

So I just keep running.

I run left. I run right. I run just to run.

It's not until I'm a block away that I realize where I've been running this whole time.

Home.

I don't know why I've come here exactly, but maybe it's to find my mother. Harry is gone—at least for now. But maybe my mother has finally returned.

I enter the house shouting, "Mom? Are you there? Are you okay?"

I go from room to room, flipping light switches. She's not downstairs, so I head upstairs, to her bedroom. Maybe she got home and fell asleep.

It's empty, just like the rest of the house.

CHAPTER
13

I don't know what to do. I'm exhausted. I'm delirious.

I collapse on my living room couch.

My head is flooded with thoughts. Am I sleeping? Am I dreaming?

No, not thoughts: images.

Of wolves.

Not werewolves—actual four-legged wolves.

Somehow I recognize them. Maybe it's their fur. The one with the black fur is Harry. The one with the extra-long, straw-straight fur is my father. My mother's fur is red.

It's them. All the people I care about. They're in a pack together. And they're bounding away from me.

I watch their tails swish back and forth as they move farther and farther away.

I have to squint to see it, but I'm pretty sure there's another tail—another wolf.

It's auburn.

It's Mara.

Mara.

I need to go find Mara.

I open my eyes, jump off the couch.

Right before I leave the house, I have one last thought: my pills. Maybe I should take one of my pills.

But I can't. It's as though my body is overruling my mind. It wants me to leave the house. Now.

CHAPTER
14

Everything is a blur.

Partly because I'm running so fast.

I feel like every stride is longer and stronger than the last.

It's the middle of the night, and the houses rush by me. I'm covering entire blocks in a matter of seconds.

Plus, for some reason, I'm having trouble remembering things. I can't remember where I've been, or where I'm going. I can't remember why I'm running.

Or maybe it's just that I don't care about these things.

I want to run—so that's what I'm doing.

Then I want to stop—so I do that, too.

I'm standing and panting and staring at a house.

Whose house?

Mine?

No.

Mara's.

The house is yellow with white trim. I know this, even though I can't actually see what color it is in the dark. There's a basketball hoop next to the driveway.

I scratch my head.

All of a sudden it's not dark out. Or cold. It's the middle of the day—the middle of summer.

This isn't real, I tell myself. *It's a memory.*

There are two kids on the driveway. They're maybe 10 or 11 years old, and they're panting, trying to catch their breath. They've just played a game of one-on-one.

One of the kids is . . . me.

The other one is . . . Mara.

Her short auburn hair is up in a ponytail. She has a basketball under her arm.

"Wanna play again?" she asks.

I tell her I'm too tired.

"Too tired?" she says. "Or too scared?"

She's taunting me, but it's all in good fun. She passes the basketball back and forth from one hand to the other.

I grab the ball out of her hands. We start another game. Whenever she makes a shot, she holds her follow-through for a couple of seconds, just to rub it in. She's really good, and she knows it, and she likes it.

So do I.

It's her ball again. She makes a jab step, dribbles to her left, then crosses in front of me. Our feet get tangled. We tumble to the pavement.

Both of us scratch up our legs. Neither of us minds.

I'm lying on top of her, looking at her grin.

"That move was so pretty," she says, "I bet you want to kiss me, don't you?"

I do. But I'm too afraid to say it.

"Sorry," she says. She rolls out from under me and stands up. "I already told you I'm saving my first kiss for Nick."

I point out that Nick's never even talked to her.

"He will," she says. "How could anyone resist these moves?"

She takes a shot. Nothing but net.

She's still holding her follow-through when someone else steps onto the driveway. It's an adult . . . her dad.

"Better come inside and get those cuts cleaned up," he says.

I watch Mara and my younger self walk into the house. The front door closes.

✦ ✦ ✦ ✦ ✦

The memory is over. It's night again—and cold. I can see my breath as I stare at the house. I press the palms of my hands against my temples.

Another memory blasts through my skull.

We're in her house. In her bedroom.

It's a few years later.

We're sitting on the edge of her bed. I'm not looking at Mara. I'm staring at her tidy bed, pressing my hand into the blanket, which is covered with pictures of professional basketball players.

I don't want to look at Mara because she's holding a bottle of Wolf-It!©.

"Can werewolves even play basketball?" I ask.

"Why wouldn't they be able to?" she asks.

"Mom says something happens to their minds. They only want to do certain things and not others."

"Okay, so I'll play other sports," Mara says. "Maybe I'll be the first-ever girl to play professional football."

"You just want to be on the same team as Nick," I say.

I'm still staring at the blanket, but Mara uses her free hand to lift my chin toward her. She's smiling—but it's a sad smile.

"Yeah, Alex," she says, "I do. I've been telling you that for a long time."

"Even if you take that stuff, Nick might still ignore you."

"Alex, he *gave* me this stuff. Besides, werewolves always travel in packs. Everyone knows that."

I try to look away again, but Mara holds my chin in place. "I don't know what you're so worried about," she says. "Your dad was Terry the Terror. Pretty soon you're going to be a werewolf, too. You can join our pack!"

Mara's still holding my chin as she drains the bottle of Wolf-It!©.

✦ ✦ ✦ ✦ ✦

I shake my head and snap out of the memory.

I look around. It's still night, but the sky is starting to get lighter. Soon it will be morning.

The time for remembering is over.

I turn back to Mara's house. I wonder if she's in her bedroom.

Probably not.

She's probably roaming the town. That's what werewolves do at night.

She's probably with Nick and the rest of the pack.

She was right, I think. *I can join them.*

CHAPTER
15

I spend the rest of the night trying to track down the pack. I dash through neighborhoods and across highways. It's not until I get to the park that I see any signs of the other werewolves.

There are footprints in the frosty grass. Lots of them. I follow the footprints into the woods and find even more. There are trampled bushes and broken branches everywhere.

I thrash my way through the woods. I'm in a hurry. The sun is out now. Soon the frost will melt, and the footprints will vanish.

They lead me through the woods. A tall, wide building looms in the distance.

It's my school.

Is my pack in there? There's no way I'm going in there without my pack.

Just thinking about it makes me tired.

I turn around and head back into the woods. I find a pile of leaves and squirm my way inside it. The leaves are wet and cold. But they'll dry out soon enough. I close my eyes and wait for sleep to come.

✦ ✦ ✦ ✦ ✦

When I wake up, the sun is on the other side of the sky. I must have slept for hours.

I'm groggy.

And *hungry*.

I look through the leaves I'm lying in for signs of prey. It must be somewhere. I can hear rustling and chirping.

My stomach growls.

When I'm sick of waiting and listening, I growl, too. I launch myself out of the leaves and bare my teeth.

But I don't see anything.

Not at ground level.

The only prey I can find is in the trees. Birds. Squirrels. I bark at them, but I know it's no use. I could climb the tree, but a pesky squirrel wouldn't be worth it.

I want bigger game.

And I need my pack to help me get it.

CHAPTER
16

It takes me a second, but then I remember where my pack must be. I rip through the trees and out of the park.

When I get to the school building, I yank open the front door.

I walk down an empty hall, growling because I feel like it.

A bell rings.

Doors fling open all along the hallway. I'm suddenly surrounded by prey.

Human prey.

Several of them bump into me as they hurry down the hall. One of them turns and looks right at me. I'm about to pounce when I hear growling that isn't my own.

That's when I see them.

My pack. They're up ahead. They're all following the white-haired one. But it's the auburn-haired one that I want to follow. She's in the back of the pack. She doesn't walk; she saunters.

I hurry after her.

I don't make it two or three steps before something knocks me to the ground. I jump back to my feet and thrash blindly with my arm. I curl my lip back and snarl.

Someone is on the floor. But what is he?

Is he prey? Or is he part of the pack?

There's something odd about him.

I try to focus.

He's wearing a jacket with a big white letter on it. It's familiar to me. But the thing inside the jacket isn't. He's big and muscular, like me. But his eyes are nothing like mine. They look confused, afraid.

I growl at him once more and hurry down the hallway to catch up to my pack.

✦ ✦ ✦ ✦ ✦

By the time I find them, two are missing. The females. Where did they go? Where is the one with auburn hair?

The remaining pack members enter another room. It takes me awhile, but I remember what this is. It's a locker room.

Nobody else is in the locker room. But there are bins in the back that are loaded with football gear.

The others start putting on pads. I do, too.

When they're finished, they head out the door. I follow them.

Just as I reach for the door, someone yells, "Dang it, Hughes!"

I turn to the voice. It's more human prey. He's wearing sunglasses over his eyes.

"What the heck were you thinking?" he says. "You should never go into a locker room with werewolves. It's a good way to get yourself killed!"

What is he talking about? Why shouldn't I be with my pack?

I wonder if he's looking at me through his sunglasses. He better not be.

I want to attack him.

I want us *all* to attack him. Rip him to shreds.

But they're not here. I need to find them again. As soon as possible.

The next human won't be so lucky.

CHAPTER
17

The noise. It's *so loud*.

I'm surrounded by human prey. Most of them are above me. Like squirrels on a branch.

They're shouting and slapping their hands together.

"DEFENSE!" they shout. "DEFENSE!"

There's too many of them to focus on just one. For some reason I don't want to be up there eating them. I want to be out there.

On the field.

With my pack.

But instead, I've been standing here on the sideline.

The one with white hair doesn't so much bark as roar.

I see movement. It's a ball. One human prey gives it to another human prey.

All I can think is: Get it! Get the ball!

Get the one running with the ball!

The one with white hair is thinking the same thing. He chases after the prey with the ball.

Get him! Tear him limb from limb!

But before the white-haired one gets there, three other human prey dive at him, helmets first.

The helmets slam into the white-haired one's leg.

CRACK!

The one with white hair yelps in pain. I wait for him to get up, but he doesn't. He just keeps yelping.

Human prey in striped shirts surround him. They all pull their guns from their hips and shoot the one with white hair.

Instantly, the yelping stops.

The others in my pack jump at the striped prey. But the striped prey are ready for them. They shoot them, too.

I'm about to attack the striped prey myself when someone starts yelling at me.

"Hughes!"

It's the human prey with sunglasses.

"Where's your helmet?" he screams. "We just lost our middle linebacker and half our defensive line! I need you to get out there! Jackson—give your helmet to Hughes!"

Before I know what's happening, someone slams a helmet onto my head and pushes me onto the field.

I hate the helmet. It feels like I can't breathe.

I pull it off. Toss it behind me. Then race onto the field.

I want to sink my fangs into the striped prey. But not as much as I want to get that ball.

It's moving from prey to prey again. One of them finally ends up with the ball and runs with it.

You're mine, I think.

I launch myself into the air and land on top of him. I go for his arm first. I bite down and tear off a hunk of flesh. As soon as I swallow it, I'll move to the neck.

I'll go for the kill.

But all of a sudden I'm woozy. I can't move my body. My eyelids are too heavy to keep open. I collapse on top of the human prey and everything goes dark.

CHAPTER
18

When I come to, I'm in my bedroom. On my bed

Someone's looking down at me.

"Mom?" I say.

I can hardly believe it. It feels like it's been years since I saw her. Lifetimes, even.

"Alex!" she says. But then her face tilts. She looks concerned. "How do you feel?"

I think about it.

"I feel fine," I say. "Like myself."

Mom lets out a big, relieved sigh. A few strands of her red hair fall out from behind her ear but she doesn't seem to notice.

"How is that possible?" I ask. "How can I feel like myself again?"

"I think I've finally done it, Alex. I've found a cure."

I make her start from the beginning. What happened to her? Where has she been?

She tells me that yesterday afternoon she made a breakthrough. She uses words like *enzymes* and *degeneration*, but I tell her to skip the science talk and get to the point.

"Sorry," she says.

Then she tells me she needed to find a place to safely test the cure. The lab was full of rats hopped up on Wolf-It!©.

"Wolf rats?" I ask. "Creepy."

When her lab partner left to go to the bathroom, Mom gave a wolf rat two shots. One was to knock the wolf rat unconscious.

"I was afraid it'd bite my finger off otherwise," she says.

The other shot was the cure. All that was left to do was wait. But she couldn't do that in the lab, so she tucked the wolf rat into her lab coat and headed for the elevator. She was worried her lab partner might get suspicious, so she spent the night on the move. Even if the cure worked, it would take the wolf rat hours to turn back into a regular rat. Mom went from room to room and floor to floor, trying to avoid detection. At some point she ended up on the ninth floor.

"What's on the ninth floor?" I ask.

"That's a secret," she says.

"The entire lab is top secret," I say.

"That's true, Alex. But the ninth floor was supposed to be off-limits even to me."

She says that she'd heard other scientists say the floor was connected with the government. Maybe the CIA or something. Maybe they trained and developed super agents there—werewolves who were even more deadly than usual.

"That was just speculation, though," Mom says. "And I needed a place to hide. So I took the elevator to the ninth floor, stepped into the room, and alarms started blaring. I hurried back into the elevator, but by then I'd seen everything I needed to see."

"What?" I ask.

But Mom is tearing up. "It doesn't matter, Alex," she says. "I just . . . I'd rather not say. What matters is that the cure worked. On the rat, and now on you."

I sit up.

"C'mon, Mom," I say. "You can't—"

I'm about to keep talking, when I see something lurking behind Mom.

It's a werewolf.

CHAPTER
19

Mom must see my eyes widen in fear, because she turns to see what I'm looking at.

It's not just any werewolf.

It's Mara.

She looks as beautiful as ever—but she *is* a werewolf. And Mom and I are staring right into her eyes.

"Hi, Mara," I say, because I can't think of anything else to say.

Her eyes scrunch up. "You . . . can . . . talk?" she says.

She sounds confused.

The feeling's mutual.

"*You* can talk?" I ask her.

CHAPTER
20

Mara nods. "We . . . both . . . can," she says.

"Both?" my mother asks.

"Jennifer."

Jennifer must mean Jennifer Beamon, the other female werewolf.

"Interesting," my mother says.

"But then, why haven't I ever heard you talk?" I ask.

I've never heard *any* werewolf talk. Except me. And that's because of the pills.

"Nick . . . doesn't . . . like it," she says.

Which pisses me off. I can't help it. Once again, like always, she let Nick rule her life. She chose Nick over being an athlete, over being a student, even, it turns out, over *talking*.

"How could you let him do that to you?" I say angrily.

Mom turns to me. "What would you do if you were her?" she says. She's angry, too. *At me.* "Nick is the pack leader. If you want to stay in the pack, you follow his rules."

A lot of what happened over the last few days is a blur. But I can remember that pull. That need to be a part of the pack.

"Are you alone?" I ask Mara.

She nods again. "Nick . . . is . . . gone."

"Gone where?"

"They . . . took . . . him."

I'm about to ask who *they* are, but then I remember: Nick got hurt at the game. He left on a stretcher. He must be at a hospital somewhere.

He wasn't the only one who got hurt, either. I look at Mom, suddenly frantic. "The kid. The one I bit. Is he . . . "

Mom pats my hand. "It's okay, Alex. He's fine. Needed lots of stitches, but he's going to be just fine."

"It was just like you said," I tell her. "My mind . . . I couldn't think straight."

"Why . . . can . . . you . . . think . . . straight . . . now?" Mara says. She steps closer to the bed. "I . . . saw . . . you . . . at . . . the . . . game. That's . . . why . . . I . . . came." Mara pauses, takes a deep breath. She may be able to talk, but it takes a lot out of her. Finally, she asks me, "Why . . . are . . . you . . ." There's another long pause before she comes up with the right word: ". . . better?"

The word is startling. She thinks I'm better? That being human is better than being a werewolf?

Mom and I take turns explaining everything. My condition. My pills. The cure. I can't tell if Mara understands every word. She presses her hands to the side of her head several times.

Then I risk a question: "Do you want to be *better*, too?"

Mara nods.

Mom sighs again, but not with relief.

"I want you to be better," she tells Mara. "But we'll need to go back to the lab, so I can make more of the cure."

"I'll help," I say.

Mara says, "Me . . . too."

CHAPTER
21

The plan is simple. We're going to go to H.O.W.L. and find whatever Mom needs to make more of the antidote. She'll inject Mara right away. Then we'll steal what Mom needs to make a big batch at home.

"What . . . about . . . Jennifer?" Mara asks.

"Will she come with us?" Mom says.

Mara nods.

"How about Harry?" Mom asks me.

"I'll try," I tell her.

Which means Mara and I need to go to school first.

✦ ✦ ✦ ✦ ✦

It's the afternoon. If we hurry, we can make it to school just before the final bell. We pile into Mom's car, and she backs out of the driveway. It's not until I look back that I see all the vehicles lining our street.

"What's going on?" I ask.

"Reporters," Mom says. "Didn't you realize? After what happened last night—on *national TV*—you're a celebrity. Terry the Terror's son is a werewolf!"

"But I'm not a werewolf," I tell her. "Not anymore."

"They don't know that," Mom says.

We're on the street now, and the vehicles are following us.

"Can't I just tell them I'm not a werewolf?"

"I wouldn't," Mom says. She checks the rearview mirror. "Not yet, anyway. If we tell them now that you're cured, H.O.W.L. will know what I've done. We'll never get inside the lab."

We've arrived at school. Mom keeps her car idling by the front door. The news vehicles park behind her.

"What should I do?" I ask her.

"Run as fast as you can into the building," Mom says. "They can't get to you in there. It's illegal."

Mara and I follow her advice. We swing our car doors open and sprint into the school.

The hallways are empty—but they won't be for long.

"You know where to find Jennifer?" I ask her.

She nods.

We agree to meet right here in 20 minutes.

✦ ✦ ✦ ✦ ✦

Harry will be in his history class—assuming he showed up for school at all. I know he was here yesterday. I remember thrashing him to the floor, but not much else.

Anyway, I want to talk to him alone. My best bet, I think, is to wait for him by the locker room. Assuming he goes to practice today, he'll have to go to the locker room first.

I honestly don't know what to expect.

Is he more wolf or human? Can he talk? This will be a lot easier if he can still talk.

✦ ✦ ✦ ✦ ✦

I'm approaching the locker room when I hear Coach Leonard's voice.

"Hughes? Is that you? I've been looking for you."

I almost answer him, but then I realize that werewolves aren't supposed to be able to talk.

And he definitely thinks I'm a werewolf. I can tell by the way his hand hovers over his tranquilizer gun.

I remember what my mom said: Pretend to be a werewolf until we get the stuff from the lab.

I scrunch up my face like I don't understand. Then I curl my lips back.

I can see my reflection in his sunglasses. I look pretty intimidating.

But Coach Leonard just smiles.

"Let's go in my office," he says.

He makes an exaggerated pointing motion to the locker room, because he thinks I need help understanding.

He's in front of me, walking backward into the locker room, being careful not to take his sunglass-wearing eyes off me. His hand is curled around the tranquilizer gun, just in case. I follow him through the locker room to his office.

When he gets to his desk, he unlocks a drawer.

"I just wanted to give you this," he says.

He slides a FangGuard© across the desk to me.

"Go ahead," he says.

He mimes putting the FangGuard© into his mouth.

I do what he asks.

"I just lost my best player," he says. He's talking out loud, but I can tell he assumes I won't understand or care. "Whoever heard of a werewolf breaking his leg? What is he going to do now? Be an accountant?" He snaps his fingers. "Just like that he goes from being the most important guy in the school to being totally useless." Coach Leonard points at me. "You're the only hope I've got left." There's a pause. "I've just got one question," he says. "How did this happen to you? I mean, if you really got your father's genes, why did it take them so long to kick in?"

I get what he's asking. *You're not a hereditary wolf, are you? You're taking Wolf-It!© right?*

Then again, I know he's not really asking *me* anything. As far as he's concerned, I can't talk. So I just sit there and chew on the FangGuard©.

Coach Leonard fishes around in his pocket and comes up with a key. He uses it to open another drawer. He takes out a bottle of Wolf-It!© and sets it on the table.

"Is this your secret?" he asks. "It *is*, isn't it? I can see it in your eyes. Once you get this stuff in you, you can't get enough, can you? Don't worry—your secret's safe with me. If you ever need more, you can come to me. Okay, Hughes?"

I chew my FangGuard© and try not to give myself away. It's not easy. All these years I've wondered how Nick got ahold of Wolf-It!©. Now I know. I'm not a werewolf anymore, but I want to attack Coach Leonard anyway.

Somehow, I hold myself back.

Coach Leonard tells me I can go. He points to the door to help me understand.

✦ ✦ ✦ ✦ ✦

The locker room is close to a set of stairs, and I crouch underneath them and watch athletes hurry by. I'm about to give up on Harry when I see a hulking kid in a red letter jacket stomp down the hallway.

"Harry?" I say.

He spins around. It takes him awhile to spot me, but when he does, he smiles.

"Alex!" he says. "I can't believe it's you!"

I can't believe it's *him*. It's not just that he's several inches taller than he used to be. Or that he's so much more muscular. There's something else about him.

Maybe it's the way he twitches. He looks both scared and scary at the same time.

"Do you have any more?" he asks.

"More what?"

"You know *what*, man. More Wolf-It!©. I saw you yesterday. You were a beast. I knew you'd come around. Your mom gave it to you, right? Right? Don't hold out on me, man!"

He's talking so fast, I can barely keep up. All this time I've been worried that he wouldn't be able to talk. But that's not the problem. He still has a voice—it's just not the same voice as before. He doesn't sound confident or smooth.

No, he hasn't lost his voice. But he *has* lost control of it.

That's when I notice all the rips in his jacket.

"Did I do this?" I ask him.

He looks at his jacket and looks back up at me. "You, the other werewolves. You all did it. You wouldn't accept me, but I get it. I wasn't wolf enough yet. That's why I need more. Come on, man. Hook me up."

"I don't have any more, Harry," I tell him. "I'm sorry."

Harry grabs me by my shirt and starts shaking me violently.

"But I can help," I tell him quickly.

He lets go of me and pretends to grab his chest. "You almost gave me a heart attack, man. Why'd you have to say it like that?" He waves his hands wildly. "Okay, okay. No worries. Tell me what I have to do."

"My mom doesn't make Wolf-It!©," I say, "but she does make a cure."

"A cure?"

"You can go back to who you were, Harry. You can—"

"Back to who I was? Why would I want to go back to who I was?" He grabs me by the shirt again. "Stop messing with me, man! I need more Wolf-It!©. Don't you understand? I've almost made it! They'll let me join their pack!"

He lifts me up by my armpits and starts slamming me against the wall. "Quit playing around, man!" He's yelling and crying at the same time. "Give me the stuff! We're supposed to be friends!"

I close my eyes and try to not think about the pain. There's nothing I can do. He's too strong. I'm helpless.

Suddenly the hallway is filled with vicious barking. I open my eyes. Mara and Jennifer are running toward us.

"Let . . . him . . . go!" Mara snarls.

I don't know if Harry is afraid or surprised. Not only are werewolves defending a regular human, they're talking.

He releases me, and I fall to the floor.

"Can . . . you . . . get . . . up?" Mara asks.

I nod.

"Let's . . . go."

CHAPTER
22

Mara, Jennifer, and I jump into Mom's car. It's still idling, so she's able to speed away before the news vehicles know what's happening. She races down the street, then turns onto a dirt road I never knew existed.

"What are you doing?" I ask her.

"Taking back roads," she says. "I had to do this a lot during the trial."

I tell her I'm impressed.

"Don't be," she says. "Believe me, they'll catch up soon enough, no matter what route I take. All they care about is their story."

She swerves onto another rutted road. We bump along for half an hour before we get back on the highway. A few miles later, we take another strategic detour.

A few miles after that, Mom pulls into her parking spot at H.O.W.L.

"This is it?" I ask Mom. "Really?"

It's just an ugly, dirty beige building. It says H.O.W.L. above the front door, but the letters are small and there's no cool symbol or anything. I'm pretty sure they're the kind of letters that can be lit up, but they must have all burned out.

"Back before the scandal," Mom says, "we had plans to move into a state-of-the-art building. But now? Trust me, when you're in the black market, you want to look as boring as you possibly can."

The four of us get out of the car, and Mom leads the way to a side door. She takes out a key card. "Let's just hope Herb hasn't reported me for suspicious behavior," she says. Herb is her lab partner. Mom swipes the card, and we hear the front door unlock. "So far, so good," she says.

We follow her inside the building. Mom's lab is on the third floor. We use the stairs instead of the elevator. When we get to the lab, she opens the door and peers inside.

"It's a good thing coffee runs through Herb's system so quickly," she says. "He must take 15 bathroom breaks a day." She motions us inside. "Come on. We're going to have to work quickly."

Of course, it's Mom who does all the work. But when she points to something—a beaker full of chemicals, a button to press—we do what she needs.

Mostly, Jennifer, Mara, and I stand around looking at the lab. The floor is tiled and bleached white. The tables are stainless steel. So are the giant refrigerators lining one of the walls.

As far as I can tell, Mara and Jennifer aren't paying attention to any of this. They're looking at the other wall. That's where cages are stacked, one on top of the other. Each one is full of rats.

No, not rats. Wolf rats.

They're huge. Extra furry. And fanged.

Then something occurs to me.

"I thought rats weren't affected negatively by Wolf-It!©," I tell Mom. That's what she's always told me.

"They weren't," Mom says, still looking into a microscope. "Not by the old stuff. These rats were injected with a new strain of calithrene. It hasn't hit the market yet—but it will. It's worth too much not to."

The rats appear to be barking nonstop, but I can't hear them. The glass on their cages must be soundproof.

It's eerie being able to see all that aggression but not hear it. Mara and Jennifer must feel the same way, because they growl back.

That's when I notice the cage with only one rat in it. This rat isn't barking. It's walking around its cage, sniffing, doing regular rat things. That must be the one Mom cured.

"Look," I tell Mara and Jennifer.

I walk up to the cages and tap on the one with only one rat in it. All around me, the wolf rats ram into their cages, trying to get a piece of me. Their cages actually teeter.

The cured rat puts its nose up to the glass and tries to smell my finger.

"What's going on?" someone says.

The voice doesn't belong to Mom, or Mara, or Jennifer.

I turn away from the rat and see a man standing at the opposite end of the room. He has a lab coat on. And he's pointing a tranquilizer gun right at me.

CHAPTER
23

"Put the gun down, Herb."

It's my mother's voice.

Herb doesn't put the gun down, but he looks around the lab. He sees my mother first. Then he sees Mara and Jennifer.

Now he doesn't know who to point the gun at.

"What's going on?" he repeats.

Sweat drips down his face.

"It's okay, Herb," my mom says. "Alex?"

"Yeah?"

"Take the rat out of the cage, okay?"

I turn to do as she says.

"Don't touch that!" Herb screams.

"I found a cure, Herb. A *cure*. See?" Mom says. I don't know how she's able to keep her voice so steady. "Go ahead, Alex. Open the cage."

"Stop," Herb says. But there isn't much force in his voice, so I ignore him.

I unlock the cage and pick up the rat.

"Show him," Mom says.

I walk across the lab and try to hand Herb the rat. But he's still gripping the tranquilizer gun with both hands.

"See?" Mom says again. "It works, Herb. The cure *works*."

Herb is looking at the rat in my hands. Then his eyes lift up. I'm pretty sure he's watching the wolf rats. I can hear their cages teetering.

"What are you going to do?" he asks.

"I'm going to inject these two," Mom says, nodding in the direction of Jennifer and Mara, "and then I'm going to go to the ninth floor."

Herb wheels around and points the gun at my mom. "You can't do that, Sara," he says.

But he lets her inject Mara and Jennifer anyway.

"Yes I can," Mom says.

"The ninth floor?" he says.

"If you saw what was up there, you'd understand," she says.

"Isn't it protected?"

"The cure isn't going to kick in for a few hours. So I'll have backup." Mom gestures to Mara and Jennifer.

There's a long pause. Finally Herb drops the gun and asks, "How can I help?"

"I'm guessing there's about a dozen media trucks sitting in the parking lot right now," Mom says. "Would you mind letting them in the front door?"

CHAPTER
24

We get in the elevator. Mom presses the button with a 9 on it. The four of us stand silently as the elevator rises.

When we get to the ninth floor, the elevator doors open and we step through them. An alarm instantly blares.

There's a security station to our left, just as Mom told us there would be. The door is ajar. Mara and Jennifer blast through it. By the time I enter the station, Mara and Jennifer have the two security guards pinned to the floor.

There's a puddle of coffee on the floor.

"He . . . was . . . sleeping," Mara says about the guard she has pinned.

The alarm is still blaring.

"Won't there be more guards coming?" I ask Mom.

She shrugs. "Maybe. But something tells me they want as few people up here as possible."

"Who's *they*?" I ask.

"Good question. H.O.W.L.? The government? Whoever they are, they don't want people to see this."

I look through the station's glass windows. It takes me a second to realize what I'm seeing.

It's another cage.

A giant cage.

Like the ones in Mom's lab, this one's made of thick, soundproof glass. Like the wolf rats, the subjects in this cage are barking.

But they're not wolf rats.

They're werewolves.

There are dozens of them—maybe a hundred.

Unlike the wolf rats, they're not slamming into the cage. They're lying on the floor.

"What's going on?" I ask Mom.

"They're dying, Alex." Her voice cracks. Her eyes tear up. She looks down at the panel of buttons in front of her. Mom presses one of the buttons and a door to the cage swings open.

It turns out these werewolves aren't barking. They're howling. In *pain*.

Their howls are loud enough to drown out the alarm.

A part of me expects them to run through the open door. But none of them move.

They're in too much pain to move.

They're so young, I think.

Most of them can't be much over 30. Some look even younger than that. The youngest looks my age. He has white-blond hair.

"Oh my God," I say. "That's Nick. What is he doing here? I mean, I know werewolves die young—but not *that* young."

"His family probably didn't know what to do with him," Mom says. "So the hospital agreed to *take care of it*."

"You mean kill him?" I said.

Mom nods.

It's awful, but part of me wishes they *had* put him down. He's in such agony.

"He's too young to be in such pain," I say.

"They're all too young, Alex."

I watch him roll around on the ground and howl, and suddenly I have a memory—a memory that was lost long ago. It's of my father. He's in the room that's now our office at home. There's a bed, but he's lying on the floor. He must have fallen off. He's howling just like Nick. Howling and howling and howling.

"What do we do now?" I ask my mom.

"We show the reporters," she says. "We let them see and understand. We let them use their cameras so others can see and understand, too."

She squeezes my shoulder. With her other hand, she takes a syringe out of her pocket. It's amazing to think she has the cure right there in her hand. We can make all this pain go away. She bends down and injects the nearest werewolf. We watch as his cries decrease.

"We're going to do the right thing, Alex. For the first time since all this started, we're finally going to do the right thing."

P.W. HUELLER

About the Author

P.W. Hueller has an MFA from the University of Minnesota. Under the pen name Paul Hoblin, he's published several award-winning YA novels, including *Foul* (a YALSA Quick Pick for Reluctant Young Adult Readers), *The Beast* (a Junior Library Guild Selection), and *Archenemy* (a Rainbow List nominee). He lives in Saint Paul with his wife, who is also a novelist.

Questions to Think About

1. If there was a drug such as Wolf It!©, do you think people should be allowed to use it to improve their athletic abilities? Would you use it? Why, or why not?

2. While Alex wants to avoid becoming a werewolf, Harry does everything he can to become one. What motivates each of them toward their different goals?

3. Do you see any connections this story has to issues in real-world sports?

4. While Alex is the main protagonist, or the hero of the story, who is the antagonist, or the villain? Is there more than one? Use examples from the story to explain your answer.

THE ALABASTER RING

When Ethan receives a box of his dad's old belongings, what he finds puts him at odds with a killer from an international crime organization. Will Ethan and his new friend, Kendra, find what they are looking for before they come face to face with a criminal mastermind?

CONCRETE GALLERY

When Keena goes missing before her big art show, Xriss knows something is wrong. He follows clues to find her and quickly discovers that he's not the only one looking. Her abusive father and a local gang are both on her trail. Xriss needs to find Keena before it's too late.

THE DARK LENS

The lens transports Alex to an alternate world filled with ghoulish creatures. When a friend doesn't believe his story about this scary place, Alex agrees to go back—just for a moment. But as night falls, they are trapped in the dark world as creatures lurking in the shadows come out to feed.

READ MORE FROM 12-STORY LIBRARY

Every 12-Story Library book is available in many formats, including Amazon Kindle and Apple iBooks. For more information, visit your device's store or 12StoryLibrary.com.